Juanita

by
Leo Politi

733482

Charles Scribner's Sons — New York 1948

Copyright 1948 by Charles Scribner's Sons
Printed in the United States of America

J-2.73(AD)

SBN 684 - 12658 - 3

ALL ALONG OLVERA STREET in old Los Angeles there are little shops.

Here the people of the street make and sell toys and pottery, candles and all kinds of interesting things.

The little shops are called puestos. They have lovely Mexican names:

"La Paloma"	(the dove)
"La Amapola"	(the poppy)
"La Casita"	(the little house)
"Cielito Lindo"	(beautiful heaven)

The shop "Juanita" belongs to Antonio and Maria Gonzalez who named it after their little daughter Juanita.

To the Gonzalez their puesto was more than a booth where they made and sold wares. To them it was also a little home filled with dear and pleasant memories, for in here they had watched Juanita grow up to this day.

Maria made dresses and fine lace work—Antonio wove bright colored baskets.

Near the puesto grew a little tree and when Antonio hung bright colored baskets on the branches the tree seemed to be filled with flowers.

The Gonzalez did not make very much money but when things did not go so well they only had to look at Juanita playing like a little angel around the puesto and their troubles were soon forgotten.

Juanita loved her mother and father. She called her mother mamacita, and her father papacito.

Juanita is four years old now.

On the morning of her birthday Antonio played the harp, and awakened and greeted her with the Mexican birthday song Las Mañanitas (little morning).

Las Mañanitas

A-wake, my dear Jua-ni~ta, pa-pa ci-to wait-ed long, Just to
wake, my love a-wak-en, lift your eyes to see the dawn, all the

bring you lov-ing greet-ings with his lit-tle morn-ing song. A-
ti-ny birds are sing-ing and the moon my dear has gone.

Juanita wore a lovely new rose-colored dress trimmed with lace, Maria had made it for her birthday. Antonio gave her a little white dove.

Hung outside the puesto were colored paper streamers which made the place look gay for Juanita's party. Children came to the party. They liked Juanita's new dress and all of them wanted to pat and hold her little dove.

"Qué bonito!" how pretty

"Qué lindo!" how lovely, they cried.

They sang, danced and played games. Juanita's mother served delicious Mexican candies and fruit juice drinks. The children were very excited when Juanita blew out the four lighted candles on the birthday cake.

"Buenos cumpleaños Juanita!"

"Happy birthday Juanita!" everyone cried.

There was laughter when someone broke cascarónes on Juanita's head. Cascarónes are decorated egg shells filled with confetti.

As days went by Juanita and the dove became great friends. Wherever Juanita went the dove followed.

They liked to play hide and seek among the baskets.

IN THE SPRINGTIME the little tree near the puesto began to bloom and the birds fluttered and twittered around, and filled the spring air with gaiety.

The bells of the Old Mission Church near Olvera Street rang oftener as Easter time came near.

Windows, arches and doorways were decorated with flowers in preparation for "The Blessing of the Animals."

The Blessing of the Animals is a ceremony which takes place every year on the day before Easter Sunday. On this day the animals are blessed so all will go well with them during the year.

Juanita looked forward to the day of the blessing because she was to walk in the procession with her dove.

In the morning of the day of the Blessing she bathed her dove and tied a bow of green lace around its neck. In the afternoon she went to the little square near the fountain where the people with their animals and pets were to meet.

Children came with all kinds of little animals and birds which looked so lovely with colored ribbons and wreaths of flowers.

Señora Carmela came with a burro. In a basket hung across the burro's back Carmela sat her newest baby, and the other basket she filled with flowers.

Ramon and his wife Salina were there as usual.

Everyone liked Ramon and Salina because they were so kind to animals. When stray dogs and cats came their way, they fed them and gave them a home.

This year for the blessing they had many animals and loaned them to children who had none.

Ramon organized the parade. They were to walk down Olvera Street to the Old Mission Church where the Blessing would take place.

Carlos led the procession with a gentle brick-red cow wearing a garland of gardenias around her middle. Juanita and the children followed in

line with little goats, lambs, rabbits, roosters and baskets of puppies and kittens.

Then came Carmela with her burro, Carmela's baby was so cute peeking from the basket.

The organ-grinder's playful little monkey amused everyone in the parade.

Trailing alone at the end came Señor Francisco with his dog Blanco. Blanco was a very old dog and this was his twelfth blessing.

Ramon with a bright colored macaw on his shoulder walked up and down alongside the parade to see that all was going well.

The golden rays of the warm spring sun glittered joyfully over the colorful parade.

Slowly they walked in silence. One could hear only the pleasant rhythmical sound of footsteps on the tiled pavement.

Antonio sat in front of the puesto and played soft and harmonious music on his harp. He played the beautiful "La Paloma," the dove song, as the parade passed by.

La Paloma

The parade looked loveliest when it entered the church patio through arches decorated with flowers. From within the church the organ played sacred and celestial music which echoed all through the patio.

From the steps of the church the padre blessed the animals, one by one:

"Bless O Lord these animals
so all will be well with them."

and sprinkled holy water as he said the words.

Juanita's dove flapped her wings as the padre sprinkled holy water on her.

Ramon's parrot did not behave too well, he talked all through the Blessing, and Ramon kept telling him to keep quiet.

The smiling padre said, "I guess this parrot needs an extra blessing," and sprinkled more holy water on him. Everyone laughed.

After the Blessing, the people with their animals and pets crossed the street to the Old Plaza, then to Olvera Street as the Mission Bells joyously rang. There was much gay chattering and everyone was smiling now that they were blessed.

On the way children played with their pets. The little monkey caused much excitement when he ran away and climbed on the trees. The organ-grinder got very impatient and the monkey crawled back to his shoulders.

Juanita walked back with Señora Carmela. She put the dove in the basket with Carmela's baby and they played all the way home.

The people of Olvera Street lived the remaining hours of this sacred day in happy quietude.

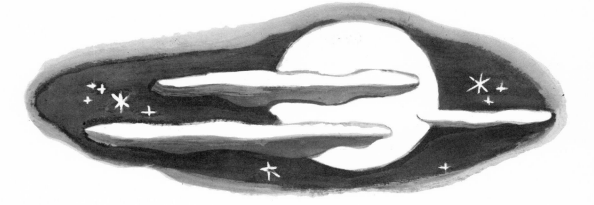

 S EVENING CAME Antonio took the baskets and toys inside the puesto, lowered the blinds and closed the door.

Soon outside all was dark except for the moonlight glow casting a silver light over the street.

Flowers strewn on the pavement were the only reminders of the lovely Blessing day.

Now Juanita rested in her mother's arms. Maria rocked her and hummed a lullaby song. . . .

Duérmete niña

Andantino

Ru-ru-ru Jua-ni-ta   go to sleep my   sweet

close to ma-ma - ci -ta   sleep my ba-by   sleep

thru the lit-tle   win-dow   in the sil-ver   night

to ca-ress Jua-ni-ta   comes a glowing   light.

Soon Juanita fell asleep and Maria laid her in her bed. The dove fluttered and perched in Juanita's arms and she too fell asleep.

Antonio caressed Juanita's dark head and whispered to Maria:

Ella es como un angelito, no Maria?
She is like a little angel, is she not Maria?

Maria hung Juanita's pretty dress neatly above the bed for her to wear in the morning to the Easter service.

And through the peaceful night echoed the joyful sound of the old Mission bells.